TRYANGEL

SUSAN HORSNELL
USA TODAY BESTSELLING AUTHOR

CONTENTS

TryAngel

Copyright © 2023 by

USA Today Bestselling Author - Susan Horsnell

Edited: Redline Editing

Edited: Robyn Corcoran

Proofread: JA Lafrance

Published by: Lipstick Publishing

Disclaimer

This story is set in Sydney Australia and written in Australian English.

Some town names are factual.

The rugby league teams and players are completely fictional and any resemblance to any player past or present is purely coincidental.

CHAPTER ONE

NATHAN

TRY!

I heard the commentator in the media box nearby scream out in excitement, but when the ref's whistle didn't sound, my nerves kicked into high gear. We needed this try to put us back in front, or we'd lose the game by two points. Two lousy points would stop us from making the grand final. Making it to the final game of the year was what every team in the league fought so hard to achieve.

The game had one minute left, and our entire season was on the line. We'd finished up minor premiers losing only one match all year; surely this wouldn't be the second.

This was it, everything rested on the decision that would be made in the next few minutes. Lose this match and we were done. Win, and we had the opportunity to play for the coveted Proven-Summons trophy for the club's first time in more than two decades. This was the first year in my time with the club that we'd even finished in the top eight.

I was thirty-four years old and had spent my entire professional playing career, fifteen years, with the Richmond Cougars. The clock was running down. If I was lucky my knees might hold out for another one, maybe two seasons. Fucked backs, knees and shoulders were par for the course in the life of a big man like me who played as a front-row prop. We took more than our fair share of hits from other equally as big men on opposition teams.

This was the best chance I'd ever had of taking the team all the way. Had I fucked it up? Had the ball bobbled from my grip as I slid to the ground? Is that why the ref had immediately consulted the bunker? Had he seen the ball hadn't been grounded cleanly, or was he just being cautious since it was a do-or-die game for both teams?

The men I captained stood around me, anxiety wafting off every sweaty body. All eyes were glued to the big screen, no one saying a word as we waited for the green light that would give us cause to celebrate. No one on the team I captained asked if I'd fucked up; they trusted I hadn't since I kept a stoic attitude and didn't allow my nerves and doubts to affect them.

Minutes felt like hours ticking by while replays from different angles continued on the big screen. The crowd was quiet; you could have heard a pin drop as everyone held their breath. Those supporting our opposition hoped we'd be denied. Our faithful followers would be crossing everything, hoping to see that powerful three-letter word that meant the team they adored had won the game.

The bunker confirmed the pass from Will Tracker—a winger was good and nothing in back play was of concern. It was only the grounding that now needed to be analysed.

My gaze zeroed in on the close-ups, shown from three different angles in high-definition detail, and my stomach flipped. The bunker called it—the grounding was clean. The ref blew his whistle with force and pointed to the spot.

TRY!

We were on our way to the grand final to be held on the following Sunday.

As the crowd erupted in a deafening roar, and our mascot—someone dressed as a cougar raced up and down the field, I was swallowed in a team hug. The ref gave us a moment before calling for the conversion. My best friend and team centre—Zane Oregon, jogged to where a ball boy had set a *Daryl Halligan Xtreme Supertee* on the ground alongside the ball. The ref blew time on, and the rest of us stood on the sideline watching as Zane lined up the kick from twenty metres out and ten in from the sideline. His leg swung, foot connected, and the ball somersaulted through the air, sailing cleanly between the goalposts and over the crossbar.

GOAL!

The final whistle was blown and the thunderous noise from the crowd engulfed the stadium. The team and I jumped around and screamed like kids in a schoolyard. We hugged, back slapped, and ruffled sweat-filled hair.

We'd won the game. We were grand final bound.

I turned to see players from the Berrilee Wolves, who had finished the regulation year in third place, slumped on the ground. Some had tears running down their cheeks. They'd been so close. I couldn't imagine how they felt and was glad I hadn't had to find out first-hand.

I gestured to Zane, our vice-captain, and with him by my side, we crossed the field and shook each of our opponents' hands. Their captain—Pedro Tarama, stood, slapped me on the back and told me to sink the fuckers when we played the following week.

We didn't know who that would be until the game scheduled for the following day was finalised. It would be either the Varroville Hyenas or the Manly Whales. They'd finished the regular season in fourth and sixth places, respectively. Both had huge Fijian and Samoan players in their front rows, which was common in all the teams, including ours. So, one thing I was sure of, the final would be a bruising affair just like today had been.

My thighs ached, both knees felt too big for the rest of my legs, and I was sure my right shoulder had almost popped out of the socket when a swinging arm from an opposing prop had clotheslined me in a big way. I dreaded the pain that would hit once the adrenaline of the win wore off.

After spending a few minutes discussing my 'miracle try,' Zane and I wandered back to our team. Various players were speaking with members of the media, but when they clapped eyes on me, they descended like vultures. This was the part of playing I detested, and it took everything in me to stay civil, especially when they attempted to invade my personal life or lack thereof.

Ewan Butler, a broadcaster from the most prominent league radio station, crossed the grass from where he'd been interviewing our five-eighth, Kovan Jackson, and shoved a microphone under my chin.

"Nathan, did you expect the win today?"

Of course, I fucking did; who runs onto the field expecting to lose? Those weren't the words I spoke out loud since the club bosses and our sponsors would not be amused.

"We always prepare to the best of our ability and give our performance everything we have out on the field, Ewan. We never take a win as a given, but we work hard to ensure we leave nothing in the tank toward achieving that goal." *There we go; I can be polite.*

"Nathan, when are you going to go off script and give me something?" Frustration was evident in Ewan's voice, but I didn't know why. He knew from experience I only ever spoke about the game. I was known as the most close-lipped, private man in the league, and I never gave the media more than was required.

The bosses of the club had pleaded with me to allow the public into my life in some small way, but I vehemently refused. I'd seen far too many lives ruined by media when they'd twisted and exaggerated some innocent comment. I was an intelligent man, a qualified lawyer, and there was no way on earth I was going to walk into their traps. I always thought carefully before opening my mouth and I'd been told it drove reporters insane that they could find nothing to target in my background. Bad luck, it was how I was and how I intended to stay. The few close friends I had knew not to say a word since they were hiding their own secrets. Fortunately, we were loyal friends and threats of consequences if any of us were exposed had never been necessary.

"I'm not sure I know what you want me to give you, Ewan."

That was a lie. I knew exactly what he was fishing for—Three…Two…One….

"You're thirty-four years old, nearing the end of your career. Do you have someone special in your life? Are you signed for next year? What will you do when you finish with football? Don't you think the public is entitled to know what you intend doing with your life once you hang up the boots?"

And—There it was. I sucked in a breath and reined in my rising anger at his rude intrusion into my life.

I smiled but spoke coldly. "What I do with my life is no one's business but my own. And no, I don't think anyone is entitled to know about my private life. You'll find out about next year when the club reveals the team for next season in a few months. Have a good evening, Ewan."

I turned away, ignoring his protests about the public wanting to know more.

"Boys...Dressing room." I shouted out to my teammates as I headed to the opening in the grandstand that led into the tunnel beneath and the team dressing rooms.

They immediately stopped signing autographs and sprinted the short distance to join me where I waited.

***

This had been a home game and our dressing room sported the blue and green colours of our team. The black cougar mascot was painted in a large circle on the ground in the centre of the space with the words 'Richmond' painted at the top of the circle and 'Cougars' below. On the left was painted the number 19, on the right 57—together the numbers signified the year our club had been formed.

Our individual spaces were painted blue and green, and our playing numbers were painted on the back wall in large white letters. There was room to hang our suits and jerseys, a small bench area to sit on, and a storage area secured with a combination lock beneath the bench. The showers were through a doorway off the far end of the room.

Mobile whiteboards that staff used to draw images of plays were pushed out of the way, and we all took a seat while we waited for our head coach—Ron White, to join us and go through a debrief. I dragged my phone from the locked area beneath my cubicle and powered it on to find texts from my parents and friends. I sent a response to mum and dad and scanned the others quickly. I'd answer those later.

"Listen up…" My head jerked up at the sound of Ron's voice. He was flanked by his assistants, Keven Bryant, and John Peacock. None of them looked particularly happy, which was par for the course. It took a lot to please the hardest men in the league.

"Nate, you came too close to fucking up today. You fumbled two passes and almost stuffed the try. Get your act together on ball handling before next week because whoever we play will take advantage of any mistakes, and we won't be as lucky as we were today."

"Bit harsh, don't you think, coach?" Leave it up to my best friend and vice-captain to come to my defence.

"Nate's your captain, Zane, he doesn't get to fuck up like he did today. It affects the entire team when the captain shows he's human."

The last comment had us all grinning, including coach which showed he wasn't too annoyed. It was hard to tell sometimes with the way he chewed us out after every game, but if he allowed his lips to curl up in a rare grin, we knew he wasn't too upset.

"Hit the showers. I want you back here for training at 7 am sharp. Linda and Janice will be here to sort out any soreness, and the rest of the staff will work with you all one-on-one throughout the day. After we work on set moves in training, I'll take you through a few things that might give us the edge no matter who we play next week. I expect you all here until the game tomorrow is done.

Linda and Janice were our physios, and at this time of the season, they were kept busy unknotting muscles and relieving soreness. At my age, I was surprised I could stay upright, let alone play a hard game of footy. I hurt and ached everywhere, but no matter how crippled I became, I refused to succumb to an ice bath. Just the mere thought of immersing my junk in ice was enough to have not just my balls climbing inside my body. Nope, been there, done that once and that was one time too many. It gave a whole other meaning to the term 'blue balls.'

The players mumbled, "yes, coach," before the five youngest of our teammates beelined for the showers so they could hit the pub. It was their last chance before training for next week commenced the following morning. Between then, and when we next played, drinking and partying were out of the equation. If they broke the rules, they were out; no second chances.

"HEY, YOU LOT!" My loud voice boomed and echoed in the confined space. All five teenagers spun to face where I stood, waiting for what I was going to say.

"Keep your behaviour in check out there tonight. The media will be like snakes in the grass watching your every move and waiting for you to do something wrong. Remember, every person on this team is needed next week, so don't fuck up and let us all down."

The *kids*—Three were aged eighteen and two were nineteen, all assured me they'd be on their best behaviour and have each other's backs. I dismissed them with a nod, and they took off in the direction of the showers.

I dropped onto my section of the bench, which was beside Zane's, and started unlacing my boots. I was sure my sore, sweaty feet breathed an audible sigh of relief when released from the boots and smelly socks. I wriggled my toes when the cool air washed over them.

"You doing anything tonight?" Zane never failed to ask me what I was doing after a game and the answer was always the same.

I turned my head and raised an eyebrow.

"I know, hot bath, a good book, and sleep. You can't blame me for asking, we hardly ever see you anymore. You're showing your age, old man."

"I see you almost every day and have dinner with you and Denise at least once a month. I don't want your beautiful wife getting sick of my company."

Zane sighed. "We better see you more often once the kid's born. I'll be expecting his godfather to be over at least once a week so you can teach him the finer points of footy."

I laughed. "Me? You run rings around me out there on the field. You're like a fucking jackrabbit, dodging and weaving. It's no wonder we have such good scoring stats; no one can catch you when you get going. Someone like me, built like the proverbial brick wall and slow, gives our opposition a lot of chance to take me to the ground."

"You sell yourself short, Nate. You are the most brilliant tactician in the game and Ron is the second best. The two of you come up with game plans that constantly blow other teams off the park. You have the best analytical mind of anyone I know, and I want my son to learn from you."

Zane had opened up about what he thought of me on several occasions since he and Denise had found out they had a kid on the way. We'd been best friends since primary school and loved each other like brothers, but only recently did I find out how much he admired me for who I was.

Pushing onto my bare feet, I slapped Zane on the back. "I'll be there for all of you."

"Thanks." Zane grabbed his gym bag, said goodnight to everyone and left to head home. Like me, he would shower once there.

I changed into a pair of jeans and a polo shirt and pulled on a pair of joggers which made my feet rather unhappy all over again. After checking everything was in the gym bag, I swung it onto my shoulder. Ron was scribbling on our playboard and deep in conversation with his two assistant coaches. I waved a hand, they gestured back, and after saying goodnight to the team, I made my way out to the car park where I had left my white Lexus beneath one of the overhead lights.

The luxury car was one of my few expensive indulgences. I tended to be what mum said was *tight-fisted* when it came to spending on myself. I just believed in saving and not spending for the sake of spending. I had a nice home five minutes from our home ground in North Ryde, my car, and enough money in the bank that I'd never have to work again. But that wasn't what I had planned.

The doors unlocked with a beep that sounded overly loud in the quiet night and the headlights flashed. I tossed the gym bag onto the passenger seat, slid behind the wheel, turned the key, bringing the engine to life and set off home. A hot bath awaited.

CHAPTER TWO

SHAUNA

Leaning over the pool table, I sank the eight ball with ease, stood and smirked at Aaron— my smart-arse opponent who believed he was God's gift to the game. I extended a hand and wriggled my fingers. "Pay up." He slapped a fifty into my palm and I heard him grumble "bitch" under his breath.

My best friend, Olivia, slapped him on the back. "Is this where I say *I told you so?*"

She had warned the newcomer, from who knew where, that I was the bar champion and hadn't been beaten for the past five years.

He'd smirked at Olivia which seemed to be a habit of the arrogant prick, offered me a fifty and told me—no, he'd *ordered* me to "rack 'em."

He mumbled something again before turning to his friend and giving a curt nod. They stalked away in the direction of the front door, obviously done for the night.

"Another lemon, lime, and bitters, Shauna? My shout, I just won fifty off the idiot's mate." Ben, another good friend, waved the note in the air, a grin plastered on his face.

"Thanks. I'll meet you back at the table."

Ben turned to head to the bar with his roommate, Joel, and Olivia shouted out to his back. "I'll have another too, Ben."

Ben gave her the finger. I had no idea what was going on between the two of them. They'd been angry and hurling insults for almost a month which was unusual since we'd all been friends since primary school and had gotten on well for over twenty years. I couldn't help wondering what had happened to set the pair off. I'd asked Olivia, and Joel had asked Ben, but neither were willing to say a word. So, the tension and outright aggression continued between the two, which made it rather uncomfortable for us all.

"I see you two love each other as much as ever. Maybe you should make up and fuck each other." I couldn't resist poking at Olivia. I'd hoped to get her mad enough to just spit out what was bothering her because I hated seeing the conflict between our friends.

Olivia's face turned red, and anger flared in her eyes. Not for the first time in the past month I wondered if mentioning the two should hit the closest bed had touched a nerve. Neither would admit being with the other, but they hadn't outright denied it either, choosing instead to change the subject.

"Let it go, Shauna."

Olivia stomped away towards the table we'd commandeered when we'd arrived and where Joyce and Corey sat playing tonsil hockey. They were no doubt also listening to loud music being blasted through speakers placed high on the walls surrounding the entire room. The two had been married for eight years, had two kids and were still madly in love with each other. It was a little sickening for someone like me who didn't believe in the emotion. But like the rest of my friends, they'd been a valued part of our group since school.

I set the cue back in the rack and made my way to the table where Olivia now sat checking her phone. I lowered into the chair beside her and put a hand on her arm.

"Sorry, I'll back off."

She turned her catlike green eyes on me. "No, you're not, and no, you won't. I've known you long enough now to say with certainty you will keep pushing until I snap, and *our* friendship ends up on the rocks."

I reeled back in shock, never having seen Olivia so—it was more than anger. She was seething and I felt her body trembling beneath my touch.

"I *am* sorry, Liv. I didn't know you felt so strongly about my interfering. I promise not to say another word."

Olivia nodded and tensed when Ben and Joel arrived back at the table and set drinks down for me and themselves. There was no drink for my best friend; she had been totally ignored. Whatever the hell was going on, it was serious.

I watched as rage shone in Olivia's eyes. She grabbed her purse, pushed up from the table, sending the chair she'd been sitting on toppling backwards, and headed for the doors. I scrambled out of my seat to follow.

"You're an arsehole, Ben."

I hurried into the night to catch her, but she was nowhere in sight. Maybe it was best that I left her alone and called her tomorrow to make sure she was okay.

I was no longer in the mood to socialise and was now furious with Ben and his pettiness. I mean how much would it have hurt for him to buy an extra drink for a friend?

I headed to the car park next door where my 1970s Jaguar was parked. I'd call Olivia first thing the following morning after she cooled down.

The drive home to my second floor flat in North Ryde took less than ten minutes, and a little over half an hour after leaving the bar I'd showered and was snuggled down in bed with my tablet, ready to read for the following couple of hours.

***

"Ambulance 334. Code 31. 19th Floor Lincona Centre. Police en route."

"Ambulance 334 en route."

I slid the handpiece back into the cradle and flicked on the lights and siren. Penny guided our ambulance past traffic that had pulled off to the left, leaving the road clear.

"So much for a lazy dinner before we headed to the stadium," my partner complained.

"With any luck we'll be able to stop off for something fattening and greasy and still be at the ground on time."

Penny laughed. "You can afford it. I only have to lick my lips at a bucket of hot chips and my hips widen by three centimetres."

"All the more for Meredith to hold onto."

Penny laughed again. "True. It's always good to know there's a silver lining."

The front of the Lincona Centre, a 19-storey building in the heart of Lidcombe that housed dozens of corporate offices, was fronted by numerous police and fire vehicles with lights flashing when we arrived. Personnel stood around conversing, most likely formulating a plan to talk down the possible jumper. I couldn't imagine how desperate a person had to be to want to throw themselves to their death from the top of a multi-storey building. I wondered how the hell they hadn't gotten onto the rooftop on a

Sunday when all office buildings were locked up tight.

Penny and I climbed from our vehicle and approached the other emergency service members. I recognised Donovan Otway, a police sergeant I'd been out on a couple of dates with a while back. We had nothing in common, but the guy was nice, and we became friends in passing.

"Donovan, what's the situation?"

"Young woman on the roof."

"What the fuck could be so bad that a young woman would want to end her life?" I shook my head.

"Fuck knows," Donovan answered.

"Do you think she'll jump?" Penny asked.

"No idea. Our tactical team got as far as the door that opened onto the roof, and the girl warned if the police got any closer, she'd jump. She got extremely agitated, so we backed off. The firies are erecting a jump mattress but we need a woman up there who she doesn't see as a perceived threat."

Donovan's eyes ping-ponged back and forth between the two of us and I raised an eyebrow. "I'm guessing you want one of us to go up there and speak with her? Where's your negotiator?"

"Stuck in football traffic, won't be here for at least twenty minutes and our jumper might be dead before then."

"Let me grab my coat from the ambo; it'll hide the uniform," I said by way of explanation.

"I'll get a mic ready." Donovan headed to where the Special Response Group truck was parked while I crossed back to the ambo and grabbed my coat, leaving Penny chatting with some of the other cops.

Donovan was speaking into a radio fixed to his shoulder and waved me over as I buttoned the coat to my throat, hiding all traces of my uniform. A small mic was fixed inside the lapel, out of sight but exposed enough that our voices would be heard.

"Have you done this before, Shauna?"

"Nope, never," I sassed.

Donovan frowned. "Maybe this isn't such a good idea."

I set a hand on his arm. "We deal with possible suicide victims as well as drug addicts, people with guns, knives, and alcoholics every day, Van. Trust me on this."

He nodded. "If she becomes too agitated and doesn't seem to be responding to you, back off. Keep her talking at least until our negotiator arrives and she can take over."

"I'll get her down."

After one last check to ensure the mic was working, I headed into the building and took the lift to the top floor. From there I took the steps leading to the roof. The Special Response Group team pressed themselves against the wall as I approached.

Moving into position at the door, I waited while one of the police officers pushed it open.

"Get away! I don't want you here."

I stepped onto the roof in the fading twilight to find a young girl, who looked no older than seventeen, standing near the edge of the building, her back to me. She was dressed in jeans and a pink jumper with pink joggers on her feet. Long black, wavy hair hung to her waist. I approached slowly, and when she sensed someone close by, she spun around. Her brown eyes were red rimmed making it obvious she'd been crying.

"Who are you?"

The girl didn't scream at me. She sounded almost resigned to the fact that she wouldn't be left alone.

"My name is Shauna. What's yours?"

"Are you a cop?"

"No, I'm not. Can I come and talk to you?"

The girl nodded before dropping slowly to sit on the rooftop, her head lowered. I took a few steps closer and joined her.

"Hannah."

"Sorry?"

"My name is Hannah."

"Why do you want to end your life, Hannah?"

"Jasper."

Might have known it would be over a boy. What was it about the male sex that they liked to break women's hearts? I gathered her hand in mine.

"Did you break up with Jasper?"

She nodded, a tear rolling down her cheek.

"How old are you?"

"Eighteen, almost nineteen." She lifted her tear-filled eyes to mine. "I really loved him. We'd been together for two years and he just decides he's done. How do I go on without him?"

"Sweetheart, I know your heart is breaking. I've been where you are, but I was with my boyfriend for six years. He decided one night that he liked my cousin better than me and wanted a life with her. They married, and when they divorced after a year, he spent almost a year begging me to take him back. Now, I'm a lot of things, but stupid isn't one of them."

"Are you happy?"

"Very. I joined the ambulance service after we split, which had long been my dream. It was something he wouldn't allow when we were together because he said it was too dangerous with so many crazies out there."

"How long ago did you break up with him?"

"We hooked up when we were both seventeen, split when we were twenty-three, and I'm now thirty-one. So, nine years ago."

"Have you seen him since?"

"I haven't seen or heard from him for about eight years and I'm glad. Having him in my life in any way would be toxic."

"You must think I'm very weak."

I shook my head. "Not at all. I cried buckets after Trevor moved out and lost count of the plates I broke by throwing them at the walls of our home. I was tempted so many times to say yes to getting back together, but fortunately, Olivia, my best friend, was only ever as far away as the nearest mobile phone and convinced me otherwise. What you're feeling, Hannah, is understandable, but can I give you a piece of advice that I gave myself?"

"I guess you can."

"Don't let him win. If you end your life, you allow him to steal a bunch of years from you. Years you could use to do something fantastic. Are you at Uni?"

"I was but I haven't been for a month. Not since we split."

"What are you studying?"

"English Literature. I want to teach high school."

"Well, there you go. I suggest you give Jasper the middle finger and be the best damn English teacher in New South Wales. Do it for you. Make yourself proud." I pushed to my feet and held out a hand.

Hannah gripped my hand, and I helped her to her feet. She stepped close and pulled me into a hug. "Thank you. I'm glad you came up and I'm sorry I caused so much trouble."

"No trouble at all, sweetheart. How about we head downstairs and let everyone know you're safe."

I followed Hannah across the rooftop and the Special Response Group team followed us back down to the ground floor.

Once outside, I urged Hannah to go with Donovan who assured her she wasn't under arrest. He explained the law dictated that he take her to the station because any person attempting suicide was required to be assessed by a psychiatrist.

Hannah readily agreed, gave me another hug, and after receiving Donovan's thanks, Penny and I climbed back into the ambulance and headed for Accor Stadium where the grand final of the NRL was due to begin in a little less than an hour.

***

Penny pulled back into traffic after we'd stopped at a takeaway shop to buy hot chips and bottles of soft drink.

"Tell me how we drew the short straw again, stuck watching a bunch of grown men knock each other into submission and then cry about being hurt?" I moaned.

"Trevor really did a number on you. I'm half surprised you didn't take the girl's hand and jump with her. Not all football players are toxic, Shauna. It's time you took my advice and put him out with the rest of the garbage you've rid yourself of over the years. You have so much love to give, and you don't deserve to be lonely. You could always come and play for my team."

I sighed loudly before shoving another golden-fried hot chip in my mouth and chewing before taking a sip of soft drink and speaking thoughtfully. "I know you're right. I know I need to dump Trevor into the 'I'm done' basket but it's hard you know. We were together for so long. He was 'the one,' or so I thought. I understand how Hannah felt. When you fall so deeply in love, you plan out your entire life—marriage, a home in a nice neighbourhood, 2.5 kids and a retirement of travelling. Then, *poof*! In the blink of an eye your life implodes, and everything is gone. You wonder where the hell you went wrong. And sorry, but if I ever get back on the horse, it will be a stallion. What you and Meredith have is beautiful, and sometimes I wish I was attracted to mares."

Penny laughed. "You've spent too much damn time at the farm, but seriously, giving your love to a male or female, the risks are just the same. There's no guarantee of honesty and trust. I just lucked in with Meredith. She's perfect. My soul mate and she says I'm hers. I'd trust her with my life."

"See, that's what I thought I had with Trevor—the cheating prick."

"Leave your eyes and heart open, so when your real love appears, you won't miss them."

"Hmm, I'm not sure I'll ever be ready to open my heart to anyone again, but time will tell."

Penny hit the indicator and turned the ambulance out of traffic into a restricted entrance of the stadium ground where we would spend the next three hours suffering through this year's grand final. I used to love all codes of football, but after Trevor's betrayal, I wanted nothing to do with any of the games.

A security guard stationed on the boom gate, an older fellow who appeared to be close to retirement, his silver hair glinting in the mild spring sun, gave us a wave before lifting the gate and allowing Penny to drive through. She pulled the ambulance to a stop in our designated spot alongside No 338 who had been tasked with looking after the players in the earlier games—The State Championship and the Telstra Women's Grand Final. Those events had commenced at 1 pm, and we were now set to relieve the other ambulance to monitor the main attraction.

Penny and I climbed from our seats and headed to where our colleagues—Peta and Mitchell sat eating and watching the pre-game entertainment for the Telstra Cup Grand Final through the windscreen of their vehicle.

"How's the day been?" I asked, resting my hand on the edge of the lowered window nearest Peta.

"Weren't needed. There were a few head knocks and a couple of minor injuries, but the team doctors and medical staff took care of those."

"Hopefully, our shift will be just as uneventful." I tapped on the windowsill when Marshall flashed up the engine. "Catch you at the bar soon." A bunch of us who weren't on shift caught up every few months at Sammy's Pearl, our local haunt. Every Saturday night, depending on work, Olivia, Ben, Joel, Joyce, Corey, and I got together. Penny and Meredith also joined us on occasion. Olivia, my best friend, and I talked on the phone almost every day, caught up for lunch regularly, and hit the local markets every Saturday morning. It had been her and Penny's support after I joined the ambulance service that had gotten me through the ugly breakup with Trevor.

Penny and I stood watching as the other ambulance drove away before heading down the tunnel to the team dressing rooms. Penny headed off to touch base with the Richmond Cougars' staff while I made my way to see the medical personnel in the rooms of the Varroville Hyenas.

It took less than ten minutes to advise them we were available and to meet Penny back at the ambulance, where she was already finishing off her bowl of chicken caesar salad.

Bright lights lit up the stadium in contrast to the darkened skies which surrounded the venue. A stage and equipment had been set up for the pre-game musical entertainment. It was a band I really liked—The Milky Ways. After they played, fireworks soared high into the sky. Colours cascading overhead for people's enjoyment with no regard for the long-term damage they caused to our environment and health.

As the smoke began clearing, the two teams jogged onto the field and spread out in parallel lines. Samantha Pedro sang the Australian National Anthem, and it was a wonderful rendition.

The players practised tossing the balls around while people dismantled the stage and removed everything. The ref blew time on, and the Richmond side delivered the first kick that sailed a long way downfield. It was game on.

I grabbed my e-reader, pulled up my latest book, settled back in the seat, and started reading. Penny loved rugby league and would keep her eyes glued on the play, so if she suspected we might be needed, I would be alerted to the fact.

CHAPTER THREE

NATHAN

Coach finished giving us last-minute instructions and passed over to me to address the team. I stood and moved to his side.

"This is it, guys. We've played hard this year to get to this point and we deserve to be running out onto that field. We've beaten the

Hyenas twice in the lead-up rounds; let's make it a hat trick. I know nerves are on edge, it's a huge game, bigger than any we've ever played before, but we can do this. We can take the trophy if we keep our heads screwed in place and don't lose control. You've all played exceptional football this year and I have faith we can now take it up a notch. Let's get out there and win this thing."

"Cougars! Cougars! Cougars!"

The chant from the team and our support staff echoed in the dressing room. I joined in, shouting loudly. When everyone settled, coach clapped his hands and instructed us to get moving.

As we left the room, me leading the team out, he and the staff stood in the doorway and clapped each of us on the back.

When we reached the edge of the tunnel opening into the stadium, I brought the team to a stop. The roars from the crowd were deafening as they welcomed our opposition onto the field first. I glanced up into the stands to find huge blocks of each team's colours. Flags and banners were waved in the air, signalling support for both teams.

"And now ladies and gentlemen, please welcome this year's minor premiers, the Richmond Cougars."

Our team names and positions lit up the big screen—

BACKS

Fullback	Joshua Peters
Right Wing	Phil Tracker
Right Centre	Zane Oregan
Left Centre	Liam Austin
Left Wing	Aslan Minuti
Five-Eighth	Kavan Jackson
Halfback	Kyra Lancaster

FORWARDS

Prop (Captain)	Nathan McKenzie
Hooker	Bronx Lazlo
Prop	Kahleh Abram
Second Row Forward (Vice Captain)	Micah Templeton
Second Row Forward	Breckett Mercer
Lock	Montgomery (Monty) Harris

INTERCHANGE BENCH

Chase Nalu	Owen Coles

Perry Oris   Dylan Ryson

18th MAN
Dean Culliver

COACH
Ron White

REFEREE
Mitchell Harper

TOUCH JUDGE
Eric Jonus

SENIOR REVIEW OFFICIAL
Tony Daner

The crowd erupted in a deafening roar as I jogged from the tunnel and led my team to the centre of the field. We lined up side by side, facing our opposing team who glared at us while the national anthem was sung.

When the smoke cleared, and while the entertainment equipment was being removed, I gathered the team for a last-minute talk.

"Do what you do best, boys. Whatever happens today, know I'm really fucking proud of every one of you."

Fists were bumped and we moved into positions, waiting for the ref to blow time on. I had lost the toss and Rory Urtiva had elected to have his team receive.

The ref blew time on, and the number one kicker on our side, Josh Peters, set the ball, lined up, kicked, and sent the leather flying high and long down the field. It was caught without effort, and as the small agile man took off towards us, we raced up as one.

***

Half time in the dressing room saw us all out of breath, battered and bruised, some worse than others. Liam was sporting the mother of all black eyes and a suspected fractured eye socket thanks to a stray elbow he insisted was intentional, but which couldn't be proven as such. All the pleading in the world from him hadn't been enough to convince our medical staff to let him back onto the field, so he'd been subbed—ten fucking minutes into the game. It had stung losing one of our best players so early.

I gulped down a mouthful of energy drink while coach shouted about the team leaving the sidelines vulnerable. He was right; all eight points they'd scored against us had been through breaks in our edges. We needed to close the yawning gaps.

"Nate..."

I stood when the coach said my name and handed over to me. "Coach is right; we need to cover the wings. Will, Astan, leave it for the other boys to cover the in-field. Don't come in unless you absolutely have to because it's leaving huge gaps that they're sliding through easily. I want all of us forwards to push harder through the centre and shift the ball out to the wings like I know you can. Let's test their edges and see if we can break them open. We're only down six points, boys...One converted try. We have forty minutes to get out there and turn things in our favour. Secure the ball. I don't want turnovers due to loose carries."

There was another chant of "Cougars" before we all filed back down the tunnel and onto the field.

***

The second half was going better than the first. We had managed to score and convert a try while keeping the Hyenas scoreless to level the scores. We had fifteen minutes left to score again and win the game without the headache of overtime.

I groaned when the pass went wide from Micah, was fumbled by Kahleb, and cleaned up by the opposition centre. Basic handling errors like that weren't gonna help us get over the line and win the game.

Everyone moved into position as the Hyena's left centre played the ball and took off in the direction of their goal. Breckett scooted to his left and took the small man down hard, causing him to bobble the ball and lose position. I knew this could be the opening I'd been hoping would appear. My heart thumped against my ribs as Monty played the ball into Abrams hands, thirty metres from our try line.

I took a pass from Abram which landed hard against my chest, causing a loud "oomph" to erupt from my throat. As I pushed toward the goal, two of the biggest men on the other side singled me out, made a beeline for me, and I knew I was in trouble. As they approached, I goose-stepped off to my left in hopes of avoiding the pair. From the corner of my eye, I saw Aslan coming up fast on our left wing.

Just a bit closer—Bit more. I drew the big men in as close as I dared before snapping a pass off to Aslan. He caught it on the run and sprinted the ten metres to the line. Everything from that point happened in fast-forward mode. The big men were committed to taking me down and had no hope of spinning to chase Aslan with the forward momentum they'd built. Their edge was wide open, the winger on their side being too far in-field to cover the distance and Aslan sailed over the try line. At the same time, a swinging arm to my neck had my legs going from under me and my head hitting the deck hard. Stars exploded in the air around me and pain shot through my skull. My teammates were shouting obscenities, probably directed at the two who had taken me down. I heard the ref blow his whistle, confirming the try that now put us in front before I boarded the express to Lala Land and it was lights out.

CHAPTER FOUR

SHAUNA

"Fuck!" Penny shouted.

I looked up from my iPad and the eBook, which had me thoroughly engrossed, to see a bunch of people milling around a body laid out flat on the ground.

"I think we might be needed on this one. He took a swinging arm to his neck, went down hard, and hasn't moved."

Penny and I kept our eyes on the scene, and when a man I assumed was the team doctor, since he had a stethoscope draped around his neck, stepped away and waved in our direction, we slid from the ambulance.

Penny helped me remove the stretcher, which we positioned ready at the rear of the vehicle and then we both grabbed an emergency kit bag.

We hurried towards the gathering and when we neared, the players stepped out of the way. The doctor addressed the two of us.

"He's out cold and we haven't been able to rouse him. I think this is more than him just being knocked silly. He went down hard, and it looks like he's fractured his collarbone. I'm worried about a neck injury since the swinging arm connected around his throat, so I've put a cuff on him as you can see." That was standard procedure in most football injuries. "He needs transporting immediately. I'll call Mercy Hospital and give them advanced warning of his arrival."

A Medi cab stood close by, and while I set up an IV in the man's arm, Penny took his vitals, and the doctor guided the cab into place, so it was ready for our patient.

"Pulse is rapid, BP slightly elevated, breathing thready and shallow which indicates he may have a throat injury that's preventing full airflow. You done, Shauna? He needs to be transported asap."

I packed away excess packaging after taping the IV in place, snapped the bag shut, and stood. A number of players wearing different uniforms stepped up and lifted the big man onto the stretcher of the cab. As I secured him in place, I asked, "Name?"

Silence followed, and when I turned back, a number of players were looking at me as if I was some kind of alien being.

"You don't know who this is?" The voice of the man who spoke had a surprised tone.

"Nope, I have no interest in football." I was damned if they'd make me feel inferior.

"Nathan McKenzie. Captain of the Richmond Cougars." The doctor informed me.

I nodded, not particularly interested in the information, but we needed it for the hospital. When ready to transport the man from the field, a number of players stepped up and patted him on the arm, some promising to bring the premiership trophy home.

Penny and I hurried to the ambulance with the medical team following. Nathan was transferred onto the stretcher and lifted into the back of the vehicle. I climbed in and secured the stretcher in place while Penny slammed the back doors closed and slid behind the wheel.

I rechecked Nathan's vitals. There was no change, and I was concerned about the blue tinge to his lips which indicated he had oxygen deficiency. I fixed a mask into place and started oxygen flowing.

Penny radioed in for a replacement ambulance to take care of the last minutes of the game, although by the time they arrived, it would no doubt be over. With lights flashing, the brightness bouncing off the road ahead, and siren blaring, Penny guided the ambulance along the road towards our destination.

I fixed my eyes on Nathan, taking the opportunity to examine his face. Golden brown hair hung loose around his shoulders, a slightly angular jaw was dusted with light stubble, and his gorgeous sun-kissed skin was perfection. I guessed he was in his early thirties, probably nearing the end of his football career. I wondered what he would do once he was forced to retire. While some players I'd crossed paths with weren't the brightest sparks in the fire and their options after the game were limited, others had become doctors, lawyers, or had engineering degrees. I wondered which group Nathan fell into.

The ambulance sped along the highway. There were mere minutes before we reached the emergency department at the hospital, and Nathan still hadn't shown any signs of regaining consciousness. That bothered me more than it should. I found myself desperately wanting to speak to the man. Why?

Strange thoughts of want filled my mind. I worried his condition may be serious with how deeply unconscious he appeared, but then his eyes flickered open and fixed on mine.

I smothered a gasp as I looked into the most beautiful, but pain-filled eyes I'd ever seen on a man. They were the colour of molten chocolate and dotted with golden flecks that sparkled beneath the lights in the cab of the ambulance.

Nathan let out a deep groan when he turned his head and attempted to take in his surroundings. One hand shot straight to his neck, and I gently eased it away. A tear ran from the corner of one eye; caused by his pain.

"Do you need something for pain? I have given you paracetamol in the IV but can give you something stronger if needed."

"No, don't give me anything!" Nathan croaked, and I wondered if there was a back story. "It's not that bad."

"We'll be at the hospital soon. Stay as still as you can until they assess if there is any injury to your neck. It looks like your collarbone is fractured, so you'll probably have that arm in a sling for a while. You have severe bruising around your throat, and your breathing makes me think there could be some bruising of the larynx."

"Did we get the try awarded?"

Typical, some of his first thoughts were of the bloody game.

"No idea, I wasn't watching. I'm sure someone at the hospital will be able to update you with the result."

Penny spoke up from the front and I noted the pods in her ears. "The Cougars won—sixteen points to eight. The try Aslan got was awarded, Josh converted, and your team took a shot at goal when a penalty for the swinging arm was given. Josh put it straight between the posts and the game was out of reach for the Hyenas. Congratulations."

"Thanks." Nathan's pain-filled eyes slid closed, and his breathing, although still raspy and laboured, slowed, indicated he'd fallen into sleep.

Nathan didn't stir when Penny and I unloaded him and signed him over to hospital staff where I knew he'd be in good hands. Before leaving, I took one last glance at the gorgeous man and said a few silent words of thanks to the powers above for helping us to get him to the hospital without incident.

With our shift now completed, we headed back to the station to drop off the ambulance. My next shift wasn't for two days, and I planned to take in the new exhibition at the Sydney Museum—*Unrealised Sydney*, a fascinating insight into the future of my hometown as imagined in the past. For now, though, a hot bubble bath and glass of wine was my priority when I arrived home. With that thought in mind, I slid into my car, started the engine, and pulled out into the still-heavy evening traffic.

CHAPTER FIVE

NATHAN

I fought my way through the darkness and blinked my eyes open to find myself gazing into the face of a woman who could only be described as an angel. Her brilliant blue eyes were locked on mine. Concern was etched on her face. I searched my memory for what had happened—Where I was.

My head was pounding. It felt like someone had taken a chainsaw to my skull and the searing pain in my shoulder had me wondering if it had disconnected from the rest of my body. My feet tingled which sent a wave of panic coursing through me when I lifted a hand and became aware of the neck brace. But I could feel my legs and feet, so it couldn't be too bad. Right? And why did I feel like someone was trying to strangle me as I fought for each breath?

Try—That was the last thing I remembered before opening my eyes and seeing the face of an angel—My Tryangel. Maybe I had died? I dismissed the morbid thought. I wouldn't have felt such excruciating pain if I had passed on to the next world. Would I?

I attempted to turn my head to better assess my surroundings. Big mistake! A loud groan bubbled up from deep in my chest when the chainsaw in my head became more like a jackhammer.

The angel laid a silky soft hand on my arm and tremors raced through my battered body. The touch was reassuring, her calmness settling any panic I felt.

I managed to figure out I was in the back of an ambulance—my surroundings and the fact my angel was wearing a NSW

Ambulance Service uniform were pretty big clues. It felt like we were moving at a decent clip, no doubt to the nearest hospital. It was my first experience of being whisked from the ground in an ambulance. Previous injuries I'd suffered had been managed by team staff and followed up with x-rays or scans to confirm their diagnosis. I was rather pissed that the first time I needed to be transported had come during a grand final game. A degree of dread washed over me as I wondered about the severity of my injuries. Would they be career-ending? Fuck I hoped not.

The team—Had we won?

The driver let me know the Cougars had gone on to clinch the premiership. I couldn't wait to get back to the club and help everyone celebrate. For now, though, I didn't have the will or energy to argue about being taken to hospital. I had to admit, with how I felt, I was likely in deep shit. Something was very wrong. I could feel it in my bones. Fear prickled through me before the fog thickened and I was drawn back into the darkness.

***

I woke to the sound of incessant beeping that marched in time to the thundering inside my head. My eyelids felt like tonne weights, but when I managed to peel them open, I immediately wished they'd remained closed.

Bright light assaulted my retinas, and I snapped the protective coverings closed.

"Nate, open your eyes, Sweetheart."

Mum's voice—what was she doing here? A better question was—"where was here?"

I cracked my eyes open a sliver and moaned when the light pierced my eyeballs with the intensity of a laser. Nope, not happening. They were staying firmly shut.

"I'll dim the lights." I didn't recognise the man's voice. "The bright lights will be hard on his eyes, especially after suffering severe trauma to the neck and head."

Ya think, Einstein? Wait—Neck? Head injury? Where the hell was I and what had happened? I had no memory of events.

I focused and drew on my powers of recall, as patchy as they were—Try—Angel—Ambulance. Bingo! I was in the hospital.

I tried cracking one eye open and was relieved to find I was now surrounded by semi-darkness.

"Welcome back, Mr McKenzie. How are you feeling?"

I looked into the face of a middle-aged man wearing a doctor's coat. When I didn't answer he continued speaking.

"You've caused some concern over the past forty-eight hours, so we've kept you here in ICU. The head trauma you suffered was quite severe."

Two days. How the fuck did I lose two days?

I turned my head to the side which proved to be a mistake—pain exploded in my skull, and my stomach turned over, threatening to expel any contents that might be still there. It settled pretty quick though since it must have been empty.

Mum was seated in a chair beside the bed, one hand on my arm. Dad stood behind her, a frown marring his face. A tear slid over mum's cheek before she swiped it away with what looked like a well-used tissue.

"Everyone has been so worried about you, sweetheart," she all but sobbed.

"Your teammates have been calling almost hourly, and I've lost count of how many calls I've taken from coaches and players of other teams. You've had everyone worried, son." Dad rested a hand on mum's shoulder as he spoke.

I wriggled my toes and was alarmed to feel tingling up and down my legs. "What are my injuries?" I directed my question to the doctor, praying he wouldn't say my career was over. I wanted to be the one to decide when I was done.

"The blow to your head when you hit the ground caused severe trauma. The impact caused a slight fracture and swelling which put pressure on the brain. A combination of drugs managed to solve the issue, so we weren't forced to operate. The severe concussion you suffered kept you out of it longer than we would have liked and had you not responded within the next hour or so, we would have been forced to consider more aggressive support. I'm very pleased to see you back with us, and hopefully, it will stay that way. You have a fractured clavicle, and the sling will stay on for the next three weeks. You'll then be reassessed and if healing is going okay, you'll commence physio."

"What about my neck? Why do I have tingling in my legs and feet?"

"There was no neck injury as such, but you suffered serious bruising to your larynx which caused both breathing difficulties and the tingling sensation. Fortunately, the swelling is settling, and you should find you can breathe easier. The tingling should also subside. We'll keep you here in ICU and if you continue to respond, you'll be moved into a private room tomorrow morning. I'd like to keep you here at the hospital for the next three days."

"He'll stay," my father stated.

I was too stuffed to argue which I knew pleased my worried parents. Besides, the season was over except for all the press commitments and celebratory functions, and I couldn't say I was disappointed to miss those. I wasn't huge on socialising and the rest would do me good.

"I'll check on you again in the morning."

The doctor left the cubicle, and I gave mum a weak smile. "What a time to get hurt, huh? We finally win a premiership and I miss out on hefting the trophy with the boys. Maybe next year? Who won the Clive Churchill?"

"Aslan, he played a damn good game and since he scored two of your tries, made three line breaks, 114 metres, and an intercept, it was pretty much a foregone conclusion."

I could always count on Dad to rattle off stats. Mum glanced over her shoulder at dad and gave me a look I'd seen far too often. Uh oh.

"Your father and I would like you to retire, Nathan. We came too close to losing you." Mum always was one for dramatics. "You're young, have a law degree, and there's a whole new world for you to explore and so many people who would benefit from your help. I couldn't bear to have you so badly hurt again."

Mum had always hated me playing football, and she saw my being injured as a good time to press home her point that it was time I retired.

"Not yet, Mum. I have plenty of play left in me and I want to be conscious the next time we win the grand final."

Mum sighed, and I knew she was about to protest, but dad squeezed her shoulder. It was his way of asking her to leave it be.

"Will you at least think about it? It would be nice for you to settle down with a nice girl and have kids."

"Not happening, Mum. Been there, done that, got the bruises to prove it's not for me."

"Not all girls are like Amy."

"I guess I'll take your word for it because I'm not going to delve into that can of worms and find out."

***

Three weeks later

I walked into Sammy's Pearl, a bar in the heart of Parramatta that my friends—Zane, Micah, Josh, and I frequented one night a week, usually a Saturday in the off-season. It was a central location to where we all lived.

We'd formed a close bond after joining the Cougars at the same time. My friendship with them was the main reason Amy and I had continually fought. She hated me going anywhere without her and I refused to allow her to intrude on our 'boys' nights out. I needed those nights to relax and unwind away from her smothering. Every other spare minute I had she insisted—no, demanded, I spend with her alone.

Amy had grown up in Point Piper, daddy's little girl who was gifted a brand-new Maserati, a vehicle that cost as much as some housing, on her seventeenth birthday. She had attended what was commonly said to be the best grammar school in Sydney before heading to university to study law. That's where we'd met due to being in many of the same classes. She'd been horrified to learn I'd grown up in middle-class Kellyville and was a product of the state school system. The bitch had barely given me the time of day until she heard I'd been drafted to the Richmond Cougars. Suddenly she'd been all over me and I'd been stupid enough to fall for her black widow charms.

It wasn't the money that had interested Amy; she had plenty of that thanks to trust funds and being daddy's only child. No, she craved being the centre of attention, attending galas and presentations on my arm.

It had taken me almost a year—I can be a bit slow on the uptake sometimes, to understand Amy was a controlling narcissist and I'd allowed myself to become her victim. During that time, I'd barely visited my parents because she steadfastly refused to be caught in a place like Kellyville and would never take her Maserati there. I suggested we take my Jeep Cherokee, but Amy was horrified at the thought of riding in such a middle-class vehicle. It took a while, but the penny finally dropped—Amy wasn't only a snob, she was a grade-A bitch, and I was grateful I'd continually refused her demands to sell my apartment and move into her home in a 'decent' suburb.

I'd walked away, something that had pleased my family and friends who I found out detested the woman. I'd been happy with my own company for the past twelve years. I'd indulged in a few one-night stands when I was holidaying out of the country where I wouldn't be recognised, and I never used my real name. The rest of the time, my hand provided me relief and satisfaction with no strings attached. Another relationship was out of the question; bachelorhood was secure in my future.

I crossed the dimly lit room to where my friends were seated at our regular table. Sammy, the barrel-built owner, and namesake of the place, waved from where he stood behind the bar. I knew a *Vic Bitter* would be coming my way within moments.

Pulling out a vacant chair, I dropped into it and accepted the beer from the young man Sammy had sent over. Reaching into my jacket pocket, I pulled out a five and tipped him.

"Slings off. How does the arm feel?" Micah nodded towards my arm.

"Yep, got the green light to take it off today and it feels bloody fantastic. Doc said it's healed well, and with some intense physio it should be back to normal in no time. I can't play for a few months, but at least I was able to move back home this afternoon. I love my parents but having Mum fuss over me for the past three weeks has been testing."

"She cares about you, and you gave her a pretty bad scare," Josh argued.

"I know, and I appreciate everything she and Dad have done for me but having her nag about giving up football day in and day out had me ready to jump off the roof of a building."

My friends laughed and my best friend Zane slapped me on the back. "Glad to see you didn't take that option."

I lifted the bottle of beer towards my mouth and stopped mid-air when movement, along with a tinkling laugh that sent shivers down my spine, caught my attention. I turned in my seat to better see who owned the sound that had my dick taking interest and shivers radiating through my body. Both were something that hadn't happened for a very long time.

My eyes collided with a pair of brilliant blue eyes that seemed familiar. I watched as she whispered into the ear of a redheaded woman who then spun around and raked her eyes over my face before saying something to the blue-eyed beauty who had me mesmerised.

The woman who had captured my attention set a half-finished drink on the table, pushed to her feet, and made her way over to where I was seated.

Setting my beer down, I stood as she approached. The woman was petite, only reaching my shoulders at best. Her long brown hair hung in waves down her back and those piercing blue eyes were framed by flawless porcelain skin. She had poured her curves into a pair of faded jeans and the pink jumper she wore showed there was more than enough boob to fill my large hands. Whoever this woman was, she was exactly my type.

She tilted her head back and asked, "should you be drinking?"

I pinched my eyebrows together. Why would she be questioning my having a beer? "Excuse me?"

She glanced at my shoulder. "Your arm is out of the sling. You're no longer on meds?"

Who the fuck was this woman who appeared to know who I was? Fresh shivers slid down my spine but this time they weren't pleasant. Was she a member of the media I detested?

"You don't recognise me?" Her heart-shaped lips broke apart in a smile and the good shivers were back.

"We haven't met. There's no way I'd forget you."

She laughed and set a hand on my arm, sending a powerful charge of want straight to my dick. "Let me jog your memory. Grand final day...Ambulance ride..."

I searched the compartments of my memory, desperate to figure out the identity of this gorgeous woman. It took a few moments before a bell rang.

"Angel," I murmured.

She angled her head and gave me a confused look.

"You're my Angel...my *TryAngel*, to be exact. In the ambulance I remembered the try that was scored before I was rag-dolled and then waking up and seeing the face of an angel...*Your* face. I'm Nathan McKenzie which you already know and I'm very pleased to meet you now I'm fully conscious. To answer your original question, I'm not on any meds so free to drink. Would you like to join us? I'm buying."

"That's one hell of a pickup line. Yes, I'll join you. I'm Shauna Kemp, by the way."

I guided Shauna to our table and introduced her to the boys before pulling back the empty chair alongside mine and inviting her to sit.

*****

"So, you two know each other?" Zane asked after I'd set Shauna up with a lemon, lime, and bitters since she'd informed me she didn't touch alcohol.

Shauna smiled my way before answering. "Yes. I was one of the paramedics on duty the day Nathan was injured. I monitored him on the way to Mercy while Penny drove." She pointed to a woman at the next table. "Penny has the black curly hair. The blonde beside her is Meredith, and the redhead is Olivia."

"Nice. Is Penny available...?" Micah's words trailed off as we all watched Penny and Meredith share one hell of a hot kiss. "Guess not."

We all chuckled. Micah was notorious for wanting unavailable women. Before anyone could ask if the stunning redhead was single, Shauna poured cold water on the idea.

"Olivia has something seriously bad going on at the moment. I have no idea what it is, and I've been warned if I push the issue, she'll end our friendship of twenty years. So, coming back to what I was going to say before I became side-tracked, please don't make a move on her."

"The guys will leave her alone, won't you, Zane?"

Zane choked on the mouthful of beer he'd just guzzled and sputtered. "Why pick on me?"

"Let's just say I know you have a weakness for a pretty lady."

Zane was a one-night-stand kind of guy like me but hopefully, when he met the right woman, he'd change his ways. For now, I didn't want Olivia to become one of his conquests, especially if she was in a bad place. The guys all nodded towards Shauna, not wanting to get in the middle of something.

"You all play league?" I noted a cold tone to Shauna's voice when she asked the question and wondered what the back story to her obvious dislike was about.

"We all joined the Cougars fifteen years ago and became good friends pretty much straight away. As newbies, we looked out for each other."

"You've been with the one club your entire career?" Shauna sounded stunned.

"Yep. No interest in playing for anyone else. The Cougars took a chance on all of us when we weren't really showing our potential and we owe them for showing faith."

Zane commented, "we all feel the same way as Nate. We'll finish our careers with the club."

"It's nice to know loyalty does exist. My experience is players are usually quick to jump ship when offered a few extra dollars. They don't know the meaning of loyalty."

Hmm, I suspected something in Shauna's past had made her bitter towards players, and I wondered if she'd ever let me get to know her well enough to prove her wrong. Did I want to get to know her that well? What happened to my commitment to being a bachelor?

I invited Shauna's friends over to join our table, and while Penny and Meredith were happy to sit with us, Olivia begged off, saying she was tired and wanted an early night. Since Shauna said she had driven, I offered to book Olivia an Uber which she accepted. Josh, who was no threat to Olivia since he was gay, something he made no secret of, walked her outside and waited until she was safely on her way home before joining us back at the table.

While the others got into conversations about the state of the economy, Shauna and I spent the next couple of hours chatting about her training to be a paramedic as well as touching on a few personal details. I was pleased to find out she had a place in Top Ryde, no more than ten minutes from my penthouse unit. I learned she had a younger brother—Brock, who was a Lieutenant in the Navy and based in Western Australia. It sounded like they were close. Her parents, who she spoke of fondly, lived in Parramatta, so in Amy's words, she was a 'Westie' like me which meant we were likely to have far more in common.

I found myself enthralled with Shauna and enjoyed her company far more than any woman I'd ever known but the evening passed far too quickly. Before I knew it, hours had passed, and the guys and Shauna's friends were ready to call it a night. Since Shauna was their driver, she felt obliged to leave, but I got the impression she would rather have stayed and continued talking.

We all made plans to catch up again the following week since being off-season, we had no weekend games. None of us had accepted contracts to play with English clubs this year, not that I could have, considering my injuries, but the four of us had made the decision to take some time off and get some well-earned rest after a hard year.

While everyone made their way to the front door, since it had been decided earlier that the night was on me, I placed a hand on Shauna's arm and held her back. She gazed up at me, her sparkling blue eyes wide with expectation.

"I enjoyed tonight, getting to know you a little. Would you mind if I gave you a call during the week, we could maybe catch up for coffee?"

"I'd like that," she murmured before handing me her phone. I entered my number and then sent myself a text message, so I'd have hers.

After settling the tab and assuring a concerned Sammy that I was fine and would be playing again the following year, I walked Shauna outside to where her friends stood talking to the guys.

Goodnights were exchanged, and I stood watching the sexy sway of Shauna's hips before she and her friends were swallowed into the darkness.

CHAPTER SIX

SHAUNA

I tossed my keys into a bowl on the small
entry foyer table, kicked off my shoes and
headed straight for my bedroom for a hot
shower. It had been one fucked up night with
four alcohol-soaked patients who brawled
until bones were broken, a female who was
being chased by the cops for stealing from a

local supermarket and ran straight in front of a car, and a gun-wielding teenager who'd accidentally shot his best friend. But it was our last call that had been the icing on the fucked-up cake.

Penny and I had volunteered to take a night shift when two of our colleagues received invitations to a friend's wedding and one was to be best person. It had been the shift from hell. Penny now sported the mother of all black eyes thanks to some drugged up punk, who was bleeding profusely from what appeared to be a knife wound, thought she was sent by his father to force him back home.

I was still hearing loud ringing in my left ear because I'd stupidly intervened to protect my partner and received a fist to the side of the head which had sent me to my knees for a few moments.

Penny tasered the pain in the arse, sending him to the ground, and a hurried call requesting police backup was answered within seconds. The drug addled nuisance was cuffed, a quick assessment was made that the injury wasn't life threatening, and within moments he was shoved into the back of the patrol car to go who cared where.

"You okay?" The taller of the two directed his question to both of us and we nodded.

"How did you get here so quick after we called." I wondered if they'd been patrolling nearby.

The tall one answered again. "This is an area with a rather questionable reputation and it's especially dangerous in the early hours of the morning when it's popular with dealers, those buying, and drunks taking a short cut home. When a call goes out for an ambulance to come here, we get one at the same time to provide backup."

"Thanks, it was getting ugly."

"You both need to get checked out at the hospital, we'll wait with you until your station sends someone out."

I radioed into base and ten minutes later two medics arrived in a support vehicle. While one drove the ambulance back to the station, the other drove Penny and me to the hospital to be checked over.

Penny's eye was found to have some minor blood vessel perforations and she was given drops to help with any bruising and swelling.

The doctor who examined me said I had a perforated eardrum that he was confident would heal on its own within a few weeks. I was given drops to prevent any infection.

Both of us were grounded for two weeks, which was totally unnecessary in our opinion, but there was no point in arguing.

Meredith had been called and after fussing over the pair of us, she drove me home before taking her lover back to the home they shared. I handed over the keys to my beloved Jag. She promised to have it picked up from the station later in the day and delivered safely into its secured parking spot downstairs.

I stripped off my uniform as I headed for the bedroom and was naked by the time I reached the attached ensuite, where I dumped them into the laundry basket.

Reaching into the shower cubicle, I flicked on the mixer tap and tied my hair into a messy bun while I waited for the water to come up to temperature. My thoughts drifted to Nathan who I'd had a long phone conversation with the day before.

He'd sent me several texts since we'd met six days earlier and it was nice getting to know the man. He was slowly breaking down my resolve to never let my guard down with another man who played football since he and Trevor played in different codes. I was beginning to think it was unfair to tar them all with the same brush. Where Nathan played league, Trevor played Union. Despite being a mediocre talent, Trevor had been all but guaranteed a place at the top thanks to the school he'd attended and his rich daddy's contacts. According to what was written in the media, Nathan had achieved his place at the top by being talented and having the guts and determination to work hard. I believed the reports. Even after only knowing him for a short time, I suspected Nathan was a gentleman who was honest and straight forward. I stepped beneath the waterfall of water and closed my eyes, allowing the warmth to soak into my aching muscles. Once washed and dried, I padded into the bedroom, closed the curtains against the rising sun, crawled between the covers and fell deep into sleep.

***

"What the fuck?" Olivia studied my face when I answered her knock at my door.

I had thought I'd done a good job of covering the bruising and swelling on the side of my face. Obviously not. I invited her in and stepped aside, closing the door after she entered.

"I'm almost ready, just need to grab a jacket."

Olivia followed me to the bedroom and sat on the bed, waiting while I rummaged in my walk-in robe.

"I don't know how the hell you find anything in there. I swear a battlefield would be more organised."

"I know, my promises to clean it up fall on deaf ears."

"Never mind. Tell me what happened to your face this time."

I grabbed a white Ralph Lauren jacket that I'd picked up at an op shop for thirty bucks; it was one of my favourites. I pulled it on and sat on the bed next to my friend while explaining about the drugged-up psychopath that had injured me and given Penny her black eye.

"Why the hell are you both still coming out tonight when you should be resting?"

"How many injuries have you seen me with over the years?"

"A shitload."

"And how many times have I allowed them to stop me from doing something?"

"Point taken. Trevor was an arsehole, no question, but sometimes I think he was right about your job being too dangerous."

"But I love it, Liv, and shouldn't I have the right to do what I want with my very short life? Penny and I are careful, and look out for each other, but sometimes things happen that are out of our control. If we didn't do something because we might get hurt, we'd never step foot outside our doors."

"I know you're right, but it pisses me off seeing you get hurt. You're such a good person and it isn't fair."

Olivia's voice wavered and she shocked me by bursting into tears. I pulled her into my arms and held her tight. Something was very wrong with my friend, and I wished with all my heart that she'd say what it was.

I rubbed her back soothingly. "I wish you'd trust me enough to tell me what's going on with you. I can see it's eating you alive."

Olivia sat back and I handed her a tissue from a box on my bedside table. She dabbed at her face and when she turned her eyes on mine, there was no mistaking the pain.

"I'm pregnant..."

If I hadn't been sitting down, her statement would have knocked me on my arse. To say I was surprised was an understatement. Of all the scenarios that had run through my mind, Liv's being pregnant was never one of them.

"Come again?" I needed to check I'd heard correctly.

"I'm almost four months pregnant and I'll be starting to show soon so there will be no hiding the fact."

"How? I mean who? I didn't even know you were seeing anyone."

"Yeah, about that...I'm sorry I lied to you so much over the past year and a bit. When I said I was working late, I wasn't."

Olivia's job as an accountant kept her busy but obviously not as busy as I'd been led to believe.

"So, who have you been seeing?"

Olivia dropped her eyes to where she twisted the tissue in her fingers. "You know him."

I wracked my brain in an attempt to figure out who we both knew that Liv could have been seeing. Then bells began ringing and a name popped into my head—Ding! Ding! Ding! We have a winner!

"Ben?! Ben is the father? How? When?" Such ridiculous questions but I was having trouble forming coherent words.

Olivia nodded. "We've been seeing each other every spare moment we could for over a year. I thought we were in love but..."

"Did the bastard tell you he's not staying around? I swear I'll kill the prick, I don't care if we've been friends for like— ever." A horrifying thought hit. "Did Ben tell you to have an abortion? Oh, it makes sense now, why you were so angry. Wait until I see the prick again."

Olivia set a hand on my arm. "You've got it all wrong. Ben would never want me to have an abortion."

"Then what the hell is going on, why are you so angry with each other?"

"He asked me to marry him."

Now I was even more confused. "What?!"

"When I told Ben I was pregnant, he dropped to one knee, said he loves me and proposed."

"I'm not seeing the problem. You said you've been seeing each other for over a year. Did he change his mind and take it back?"

Olivia shook her head and a tear trickled over her cheek. "No. I said no, and he stormed out before I could explain. He hasn't spoken to me since."

"Why on earth did you say no? Do you love him?"

"With all my heart."

"Okay, Liv, I know I'm not the sharpest screwdriver in the toolbox sometimes, but you've got me confused. I don't understand why you refused his proposal."

"We've been seeing each other for over a year, and he never once hinted that we should get married. He tells me all the time how much he loves me and does things all the time that show his love, but not once did marriage enter into the equation."

"Did you want him to ask you?"

"Of course, I've been in love with that man since high school and if he'd asked before he knew I was pregnant I wouldn't have hesitated to say yes. But, Shauna, if I say yes now I'd be forever wondering if it was something he truly wanted or if he'd asked only because he had some fucked-up idea about it being the right thing to do since I'm carrying his baby. I love him too much to risk having him feel trapped."

"Have you told him this?"

Olivia shook her head. "You've seen how he is, he can barely be in the same room as me let alone have a conversation."

"Then you need to force him to hear you out."

"How? He hangs up on me if I call him at work and he sends me to voicemail on his mobile. I've been around to his unit, and if he's there alone, he refuses to answer the door. If Joel's home, I can't get past him. The one time I cornered him coming out of the men's room at the bar, he got really angry and said he got the message the first time and didn't need to be told no twice. He said he didn't understand how I could throw everything we had away, and I could fall off the face of the earth as far as he was concerned." Tears tumbled over Olivia's cheeks, as her heart broke. "It hurts, Shauna, I love him so much. I want us to be together but can't bear to think he's being pushed into something without a choice."

"I understand and I have an idea that will make him realise how much you mean to him. It's a little childish and a bit unfair but it might force him to listen to what you have to say."

"I'll try anything, I want us to at least be friends even if he doesn't want anything more."

I explained my idea to Olivia who was a little hesitant at first, not wanting to upset Ben, but since it appeared she was out of options, she agreed to the plan.

"I'll call Dad and let him know you'll be dropping by shortly to pick up the keys to the holiday unit in Kiama and that you'll be staying there for a few days. Just be careful driving down and text me when you arrive. Don't answer any calls or texts from Ben, make him come to you."

"I hope this works."

"It will. Ben's a stubborn bastard but he obviously loves you."

I walked Olivia to the door, grabbed my purse and keys and we headed downstairs to where her car was parked. We hugged, she slipped behind the wheel, and while I watched her drive away, I ordered an Uber to take me to the bar where I'd meet up with Penny, Meredith, Ben, Joel, Nathan, and his friends. Operation Talk to Olivia would then commence."

CHAPTER SEVEN

NATHAN

I braced myself as I waited for Shauna who had texted me that she was running a little late since her Uber had been delayed. I'd offered to go and get her, but she'd refused so I'd stayed at Sammy's.

Penny and Meredith had arrived fifteen minutes earlier, the former sporting a black eye and swollen cheek that any league player would have been proud to show off—We're a bit strange like that.

Zane, Josh, and Micah were sitting with me at two tables we'd pushed together in readiness for Shauna and her friends. At the thought of seeing her again, my stomach had a butterfly performance happening that was worthy of any circus. What was it about the woman that had me feeling like a schoolboy with a giant-sized crush?

Penny introduced us to two men who accompanied her and Meredith that hadn't been with them the previous week—Ben and Joel. After we all shook hands, Ben made his way to the bar to order drinks. While he was gone, Joel explained how the he and Ben had also been at school with Shauna and Olivia. I felt a little jealous on hearing the men had known Shauna for so long, but the feeling quickly disappeared when I realised, if something was going to happen between my lady and one of them it would have happened well before now.

Once everyone was seated with drinks, Penny answered the question we'd all been busting to ask but hadn't. She told us about the attack on her and Shauna the previous night and blood ran cold down my spine. The ladies could have been much more badly injured, even killed! Shauna hadn't mentioned a word about the attack in her texts, if she had I would have demanded to see she was okay. I figured maybe she wanted to explain in person.

Relief washed over me when Shauna entered the bar and I saw her approaching looking as gorgeous as ever. Although I could see that one side of her face was lightly bruised and swollen, it wasn't as bad as my mind had been conjuring for which I was grateful. I stood when she came closer and studied her face beneath the dim lights. Makeup covered the bruise, and I imagined it was probably worse than what I could see but she was upright and the smile she gifted me assured me she was doing okay.

We'd been texting back and forth all week and had spoken on the phone a couple of times, learning a little more about each other and our lives. I couldn't deny that I liked the woman and felt a strange attraction towards her. One I hadn't felt before.

Acting on instinct, I leaned forward and placed a light kiss to her damaged cheek. "I want to kill the bastard who hurt you," I whispered in her ear. She placed a hand on my arm and our eyes locked.

"He was out of his mind on drugs and I'm fine. Penny copped the worst of it, but she'll be all right too. It goes with the job, Nathan."

I knew ambos, firies, and cops got hurt in one way or another all the time. It was totally unacceptable when they were only doing their jobs and trying to help. It particularly pissed me off that it had happened to Shauna and Penny, but if I wanted a chance with Shauna, I knew it was something I'd have to come to terms with and try not to worry too much.

I pulled out a chair and while Shauna sat, I crossed to the bar to get my lady a drink. First she's my woman then my lady—Interesting.

When I returned to the table I set Shauna's drink in front of her and sat down, close enough that our thighs touched, which sent fireworks cascading through every limb of my body.

"Where's Liv, wasn't she supposed to come with you?" Joel asked Shauna.

Shauna shrugged before sipping her drink.

"What's that supposed to mean? Where is she?" It sounded like Ben was concerned and I wondered if the two were together in some way.

"I have no idea. When I spoke to her earlier she sounded really upset and said she was going away."

Ben sat forward and when he spoke his tone was more demanding. "Where is she, Shauna?" Judging on the tension in his body and what appeared to be a touch of fear, I had no doubt there was definitely history between Olivia and Ben.

"She's not answering her phone so I guess she wants to be left alone and after the way you've been treating her, I can't say I blame her wanting to get away. She's a big girl and can take care of herself but I have to admit, her distress when we last spoke, and now not answering my calls is a worry."

"Fuck!" Ben dragged his fingers through his hair causing it to stick up in all directions.

The rest of us sat quietly as the exchange between him and Shauna played out.

"Do you think she's okay? Fuck...I should have taken her calls and listened when she wanted to talk but I so damn angry with her." Ben pulled a phone from the pocket of his jacket, pressed a button, and lifted it to his ear. The call went to voicemail, and he left a message begging Olivia to call him.

He pushed up from the table. "I'm going to check her place."

"She's not there. When I spoke to her a while ago she was in her car. She hung up on me after saying she was going away because she didn't want to damage Ben's friendship with the rest of us and it would be best if she was gone."

Ben dropped back into his chair, set his elbows on the table, and dropped his head into his hands for a moment before again sitting upright and pleading with Shauna.

"Please tell me she won't do anything stupid, I know I've been a dick."

"Yeah, you have been, Ben. She only wanted a chance to explain, and you've treated her like shit. I guess she took your *"I wouldn't care if you fell off the face of the earth,"* seriously."

"I didn't mean it, she said no, Shauna." Ben sounded devastated.

It was quite the drama playing out, one it seemed none of the rest of us had a clue about, and we were all engrossed.

"She had a good reason, Ben, and you would have understood if you'd given her a chance to explain. Instead, you acted like a spoiled brat who was pissed off because you couldn't get your own way," Shauna snapped.

"She told you?"

"Yes, but only just before she left."

"Will someone tell us what the fuck you two are talking about?" Joel snapped.

Ben sighed. "Liv and I have been seeing each other for a little over a year. It got serious. We love each other, or I loved her. She was everything to me, but I guess she didn't feel the same way."

"She loves you more than life, Ben," Shauna interjected.

"Then why did she say no?"

"For fuck's sake, what did she say no to?" Joel demanded to know.

"Liv told me she's pregnant about a month ago and I asked her to marry me—she said no. That's why I've been so fucking angry with her. She brushed me off like I meant nothing."

"That's not fair, Ben. Liv didn't brush you off, she tried to explain, and you wouldn't give her the chance," Shauna argued.

Joel shook his head. "You are such a stupid fuck sometimes, man."

"Huh?" Ben was confused but I knew exactly what Joel meant.

Joel shook his head. "Olivia tells you she's pregnant and the first thing you do is ask her to marry you?"

"Yeah, what's wrong with that? I love her and she's carrying our baby."

I joined in on straightening Ben out. "I don't know Olivia but if she said no, she's obviously a decent lady. Had you even hinted at wanting to marry her before then?"

"Well, no, but I would have thought about it and asked her eventually."

Shauna continued. "Think about it, Ben."

Ben's eyes widened as the penny dropped, but before he could say anything, Shauna spoke again.

"Liv didn't want you to feel trapped, she knew you'd resent her as time went on if you did something you weren't ready for. She loves you and wouldn't pressure you into marriage for any reason. That's what she's been trying to explain."

"Fuck. I need to find her. I need to tell her it really is what I want."

Even I could see Ben wasn't getting the message.

Shauna shook her head. "You don't get it, Liv won't say yes while she has doubts that you're only offering because she's pregnant."

"But I'm not. I swear it's what I've wanted for months, maybe years, because I've loved her since we were in high school and have always wanted to share my life with her. I swear it's not something I'd regret."

"It's not me you need to convince, Ben."

"If I don't know where she is, how can I make things right?"

Shauna reached into the pocket of her white jacket and pushed a slip of paper across the table towards Ben. He picked it up and studied what was written, which from where I sat looked like an address.

"Your holiday unit?"

"Yep. She's on her way down there now to spend a few days. I swear if you hurt her again Ben, they won't find your body.

"I'm with Shauna and being a cop, I know exactly how to make you disappear without a trace."

We all chuckled at Joel's threat. Ben pushed up from the table. "I won't hurt her, I give you my word I'll make things right. Thanks." Ben leaned over and kissed

Shauna's cheek before he left the bar in a hurry.

"Well, that was unexpected entertainment. So, Liv is pregnant," Penny mused.

"Yep, four and a half months so we better start gathering things for our niece or nephew." Shauna turned her face to mine. "We're all like brothers and sisters so we'll be considered aunts and uncles to this kid."

I nodded. It impressed me that Shauna had such a tight circle of friends.

CHAPTER EIGHT

NATHAN

The rest of the night was spent chatting about nothing in particular, each group of friends getting to know each other. It was friendly, relaxing, and to be honest, it was nice to start developing friendships outside football, something I hadn't experienced since I'd elected to keep to myself in the spare time I had outside training and playing.

A hand on my shoulder when I was mid-conversation had me stiffening and I turned to find a man I couldn't stand smirking down at me.

"Remove your hand from my shoulder, Ewan."

He hesitated for a moment, but probably thinking better of upsetting a man of my size, considering he was a short, skinny, weasel, he dropped it to his side.

"Are you going to introduce me to your friends." He raked his eyes over Shauna as he spoke, and my hands fisted.

"No, I am not so you can..."

"Who are you?" Shauna interrupted.

Ewan started to extend his hand until I growled, and he thought it was probably a bad idea.

"He's media scum who makes a living out of sprouting lies about people." Zane spat.

Shauna's eyes narrowed. "Oh, I know the type, we deal with the vultures at accident scenes regularly." She pierced Ewan with a glare that should have had his balls seeking refuge inside his body. "Why do you think it's okay to intrude on the privacy of someone while they enjoy a quiet night out with friends?"

"It's news. The public want to know about Nathan and he won't speak to anyone despite being public property."

My anger spiked, I'd heard Ewan make that comment far too often, but when Shauna grunted, stood, and moved to stand face to face with the arsehole, I decided to let things play out. I crossed my arms and waited for their exchange, confident Shauna was more than capable of holding her own.

She stepped forward and they were now toe to toe. "Mr McKenzie to you, is not and never will be *public property*. Football is, the man is not! His private life is his own and none of yours, or anyone else's fucking business. I suggest you leave before we encourage him to call the police and have you charged with harassment. I have no idea why he hasn't taken out a restraining order against you since it appears obvious you have no respect, but trust me when I say, I'll be strongly encouraging him to do so after tonight. Goodnight."

Ewan glared my way, I shrugged a shoulder and after one last glance at Shauna, he stormed from the bar. As Shauna sat down we all clapped. I'd never been so damn proud. It was obvious she was no shrinking violet and my first impression that she was soft, even a push-over, could not have proved to be further from the truth.

"Does he bother you as often as I think?"

"He stalks us all the time. He commentates on games and has a talk show about league on the radio. The media hounds have no respect for our privacy. Nate cops it the worst because he's the captain and they would love nothing more than to dig up dirt on someone in charge. Nate gives them nothing and there isn't anything in his past they can twist. It frustrates hell out of them. Over the years there have been outright lies printed about us, but we keep our mouths shut and don't lower ourselves to their level. We're happy to talk at conferences after games, about the game, but have told them a thousand times that our private lives are strictly off-limits." Micah hated the media almost as much as I did and with good reason after what had happened in the past, but that was his story to tell, not mine.

"I don't get it—just because a person plays sport at the elite level doesn't give anyone the right to think your private lives are up for grabs."

"Sounds like you're not a fan either." I had the strong impression Shauna had a history with the media that caused her anger.

"We detest them," Penny answered. "Some of the less moral media turn up at accidents and take photos with no regard for the victims or their families. Far too many families find out their loved ones are dead or hurt from the monsters airing the information before the police even get a chance to inform them. A couple of the vultures get in the way when we're trying to administer treatment and if a victim is conscious they'll even start asking questions. Fortunately, the cops move them along. They say the public has a right to know, seems their excuse for everything they do. My response is the public has no fucking right to anyone's life!"

Okay, Penny was definitely not a fan but to be fair, the majority of media weren't like Ewan, they were decent people and respected our requests.

The rest of the night was uneventful, and since I'd only been drinking soft drink as we were in training all year round and alcohol wasn't good for conditioning, I offered to drive Shauna home knowing she'd caught an Uber to the bar. She'd happily agreed.

After saying goodnight to our friends, I led Shauna to my Jeep, unlocked the vehicle,

98

waited for her to climb into the passenger seat, and closed the door as she buckled her seatbelt.

She gave me directions to an area I knew fairly well, and I turned into a tree-lined street that had some homes dating back to the 19th Century. I slowed and soaked in the architecture I loved that was partially lit up by the streetlights. The homes were from the Victorian era with wide front porches and decorative filigree wrought iron. The blocks they sat on were probably the traditional quarter acre, common back in the day.

"It's the next building on your left, you can park on the street out front."

I pulled off to the side of the road and left the engine idling, hoping she might invite me inside.

Shauna unbuckled her seatbelt and placed a hand on the door handle before turning to ask, "would you like to come up for a coffee?"

"I'd like that very much." I turned off the engine and the soft ticking of the motor cooling echoed in the quiet night as we both slid from the car. I locked up and joined her on the footpath in front of the small unit block.

The building was exquisite, a 1920s vintage Art Deco build, the rendered concrete exterior was painted white, and the Art Deco trims were highlighted in a jade colour. Four white edged sash windows were evenly placed across the front of both the ground and first floors. The ground floor differed with having a white painted door in the centre flanked by narrow leadlight glass windows. I found myself impatient to see inside.

"Four units, two up, two down?" I asked.

We headed towards the front door where Shauna keyed a code into the pin pad off to one side and pushed it open.

"Yes. It was built in 1925. All have three bedrooms, ensuite off the main and on the first floor a large balcony off the master suite. Downstairs opens onto a small garden area that they share. My unit is on the first floor since I have no requirement for a garden. I work far too much to put in the time it deserves, and I have a poisonous thumb when it comes to plants."

I chuckled as she led me into a well-lit, spacious entry foyer and I ensured the door closed behind us. The foyer was impressive with white painted walls, soft blue painted chair rails, marble floors and typical Art Deco frosted glass sconces were placed at even intervals on the walls. There was also recessed lighting overhead which highlighted the stairway.

Shauna took the steps ahead of me and when we reached the top, she turned to a white painted Corinthian style door on the right with a brass knocker in the center and a huge number 4. She unlocked and flipped on a light switch, flooding the area we stepped into with light. I smothered a gasp, the place was incredible.

Shauna spoke as she threw her keys in a bowl on a round wooden table in the small entry. "The entire block was renovated just before I bought my place three years ago. All the Art Deco features were restored. It's not everyone's choice of décor but it suits my tastes."

I walked into a larger space, taking in the surroundings. The kitchen lay directly ahead of a large single space. The living area to the right, dining to the left.

The kitchen was in beige tones and had off-white Art Deco block pattern upper and lower cupboard doors and drawer fronts with silver-coloured metallic handles along the width of one wall. The island bench ran almost the width of the space with a sink at one end. All benchtops were off white with a gold vein wandering randomly through the marble. A huge oven/cooktop were perfect for entertaining, and I wondered how often Shauna had someone special visit. There was plenty of cupboard and drawer space for even the most accomplished cook. Three frosted glass pendants hung on metallic chains to spotlight the benchtop. A microwave and coffee machine were inserted into custom made spaces. The back splash featured jade-coloured tiles with a large Art deco tiled motif in white.

I turned to the dining area and smiled. Shauna had exquisite taste. An L-shaped booth type seat was upholstered in jade coloured fabric, the table was dark, almost black wood, and on the opposite side of the bench were three dark timber chairs. The sideboard was made of the same wood with three glass fronted doors that were etched with an Art Deco motif. On top sat numerous jade miniatures of animals on white crocheted doilies.

The living area maintained the theme of dark wood through the coffee table, side tables and television entertainment unit. The lounge suite had a three-seater lounge flanked by two individual matching chairs. They were upholstered in jade fabric and had metallic legs. They look terribly uncomfortable but were perfect additions to the unit.

Two frosted glass pendants hung over the dining table while the walls on each side of the entertainment unit featured frosted glass sconces. Overhead, the ceiling had numerous recessed lights to brighten the entire space.

Bright prints of birds, a tiger, and swan were placed on walls with lights positioned to highlight the works of art.

On the marble floor was a large white rug and gold curtains edged in jade were held back with jade toe backs.

I felt as if I had stepped back in time, to an era where I belonged. My mother had always said I was an old soul who she was convinced had been here before. If I had, I'd been a person of the 20s.

Shauna pointed out there were two bedrooms off to the right and I noted the two closed doors on the living area wall. Beside the kitchen space were doors that led to a laundry and bathroom. To the left, she said the door opened into the master suite which had a large walk-in robe, ensuite and French doors that opened onto a spacious balcony. She didn't offer to show me, and I didn't ask.

"I'll get our coffee, have a seat."

Shauna pointed to the couch and lowered myself to a cushion on one end, preparing for it to feel like I was seated on concrete. I was pleasantly surprised when I sank down and the cushion wrapped around me like a cloud. This was a couch I could have happily slept on if necessary.

The aroma of coffee filled the room as the coffee machine bubbled and spat. Within moments, Shauna joined me with a tray in her hands.

"Caramel flavour, is that okay?"

She set the tray holding two mugs of black coffee, a small jug of milk, pot of sugar and bowl of chocolate balls on the coffee table in front of where I sat. She then joined me, sitting in the centre of the couch.

"Perfect, thank you."

"Milk or sugar?"

"Only milk."

Shauna poured milk into both mugs before offering me one along with the bowl of chocolate balls. I helped myself to two, chocolate was my weakness. Shauna didn't take one before setting the bowl down and picking up a mug for herself.

"They're chocolate, caramel balls that I make because they complement the caramel coffee."

I popped one into my mouth, bit into the chocolate and gooey caramel exploded on my tongue. I moaned as my mouth was assaulted by the decadent flavours before chewing and swallowing. I wasted no time in devouring the second treat, it was every bit as good as the first and elicited another moan.

Shauna laughed. "That good, huh?"

"I could literally eat myself to death on them. Do you cook much?"

"A bit, but not as much as I'd like because I'm so busy with work. I try and have Liv and my friends over at least once a month for dinner. I'd love it if you would come to the next one next Friday night."

"I'll be here, thank you."

"Do you cook?"

"A little, but like you, I don't have much time during the season with games, training, and conditioning."

"How's the shoulder doing?"

"Good. I've actually been cleared to start back at light training from Monday."

"Be careful, it'll be weak for a while."

"Yeah, I'll take it easy, and the staff will keep a close eye on progress. I've got one, maybe two seasons left in me, and I'd like to see them out."

I finished the delicious coffee and put the mug on the tray where Shauna had placed hers. I then shimmied closer to where she sat and took her hands in mine, staring deep into her eyes.

"Shauna?"

"Yes?" Her voice was barely a whisper and when she licked her lips, my dick flinched behind the zipper of my pants.

I brushed my fingertips lightly down the side of her bruised cheek and she leaned into the touch.

"I'd very much like to kiss you."

"I'd very much like that."

Having Shauna's permission, I wrapped her in my arms and my lips crashed down on hers. Our tongues wove in an intricate pattern of dance as I savoured her taste—Coffee and caramel. The scent of violets wafted up my nose. Shauna was as intoxicating as I'd suspected, and I was drunk on the woman. If we hadn't needed air, I would have fused my lips permanently to hers.

I pulled back but kept my arms firmly wrapped around her waist. Her eyes were glazed, pupils blown with lust.

"I'd very much like to see you—wine and dine you."

"I'd very much like that." Shauna agreed.

I wanted to drag Shauna to the bedroom, strip her naked, ravage every gorgeous inch of her and bury myself deep in her sexy body. But that would have to wait.

Shauna was not a one-night stand, someone to conquer before beating my chest in victory like a caveman. She was special and deserved to be treated as such. Every inch of her should be savoured. I suspected she would become my sun rising in the morning and the moon rising at night. I was so incredibly gone for this woman. I knew in my heart that Shauna was my future, and I would do nothing to jeopardise that future.

CHAPTER NINE

NATHAN

Grand Final Day the following year.

I laced up my boots while coach gave the team his final instructions. Our team, with all the same players as the previous year, had made it the grand final again.

"The Kellyville Koalas only just scraped into the final by the skin of their teeth but don't underestimate them. You are all aware they finished in 8th in the regular season and it's rare that a team makes it to the grand final from that position. It's even rarer that they win. They've copped shit all year because of their up and down form and are ready to shove it up their critic's arses by going all the way. Just keep in mind what we've spoken about. Nate."

I stepped into the middle of the room and scanned the faces of my teammates. "Coach is right. The Koalas have got nothing to lose and no pressure to win, so although the odds are against them, they'll give this game everything.. We're the defending champions and while half the footy population say we can't go back-to-back, the other half is expecting, almost demanding, we win since we are playing what the media have dubbed the lesser team. Let me stress this and ensure you listen—they are not the *lesser* team! They have fought hard to get here today. Don't get cocky and ensure your ball handling is spot on. Keep the fumbles to an absolute minimum. Watch their forward pack, they outweigh ours by 60kg. They are all big men and will put your lights out before you see what's coming."

Coach continued. "Like we discussed, don't spend your time trying to gain metres through the middle, we'll be slaughtered if we play the game to suit them. As Nate said, they're big men and like those on our team, they're slow, and even slower to change direction. Take advantage of that fact. Move the ball through hands fast and open them up on the wings. That's been their weakness every game this year. It's the only vulnerable part of their play, and other teams haven't capitalised and taken advantage. I'm proud of every one of you boys and I know by game's end, you'll have left everything you have on the field. Get out there and play for the eighty minutes I know you are all capable of, show them all what you are made of."

We all bumped fists before I led the team from the dressing shed, down the tunnel and onto the field. A deafening roar erupted as we appeared, and I ran the men across the field and into line for the national anthem.

We stood and mouthed the words as Sharni Bellingham sang the song that represented our country and was one we all respected.

When she sang the final note, the boundaries exploded in colourful fireworks. I looked up towards the VIP section where I knew my gorgeous wife, Shauna would be sitting with her best friend Olivia and her partner, Ben. They'd organised Ben's mother to babysit our goddaughter, Renee, so they could watch the game. Shauna and I had married three months earlier and baby McKenzie was on the way, due to be born in five months' time.

I hadn't told the team that this was my final game. After discussing it with Coach and management, I declined to sign a new contract and asked them to keep the information to themselves until after the grand final. They'd readily agreed after I explained I didn't want the men to feel pressured to send me out on a win. Men under pressure made mistakes.

I waved in the direction of Shauna knowing she'd see me even though I had no hope of seeing her thanks to the blinding lights illuminating the field. Once the field was cleared, the ref called me and the Koalas' captain over for the coin toss. I won and elected for us to receive.

The ref blew his whistle, and the kickoff was high, long, and straight down the throat of Zane whose hands were the most trustworthy in the game. He had no trouble taking the high ball before taking off down the sideline like a jackrabbit. A flick pass to Josh, as two big men bore down on Zane, found its mark and Josh continued pushing forward. The ball snapped through four more sets of hands, covering the width of the field to the right wing where it was snatched up by Will. He was just five metres out with the Koalas' small men coming up fast. Will was just too quick. He scurried over the line and planted the ball just two metres away from the right goal post and three metres deep.

Ref blew the whistle immediately indicating there was no doubt the try had been scored. We were in front 4-0 three minutes after time on had been blown. Liam converted without effort and added the extra two points. The crowd roared. It was a damn near perfect start.

***

We trudged into the dressing sheds, our forward pack, including me, feeling battered and bruised after spending the first forty minutes running interference with the Koalas' big men so our smaller men could stay out of harm's way and keep scoring points.

The score was 24-4 in our favour, a great half-time lead but we had to make sure we didn't become over-confident and throw the game away.

I flopped down in my space and guzzled what seemed like enough water to fill the average backyard swimming pool.

Coach paced back and forth talking about a couple of our errors and weaknesses he'd seen in the other side. Some of our men took the opportunity to get injections into painful joints, while others had sore muscles massaged.

After giving my team a pep talk, the last one I'd ever give, we headed back onto the field for my final forty minutes of football.

***

Nerves assaulted me, we were at the same stage of the game as last year when I'd been hurt.

I jogged up centre field, watching as Josh side-stepped the opposition, cut in field, and planted the ball dead between the posts. The game had already been out of reach, but the final try was sweet. The final siren sounded as the ref blew his whistle and indicated the spot where the ball had been grounded. We had a quick celebration on the sideline while Liam lined up the ball and nailed the conversion.

We were all over each other, the Koalas a collapsed heap on the ground. They'd given their all but just hadn't been good enough. We'd outplayed them everywhere and won 46-4, an outrageous imbalance for a grand final but we wouldn't complain.

We dropped to the ground near the presentation dais, waiting while preparations took place. Once complete, the officials began with short speeches—thank fuck.

I tuned out, thinking about what I was gonna tell the boys once we were back in the shed. I would not allow them to find out through the speech I made in acceptance of the Proven-Summons trophy or at the media conference that followed. No, they deserved for me to tell them personally and privately so they wouldn't be blindsided.

I tuned back into the speeches when the ref and touch judges were called forward and clapped as they received their medallions.

Next was the announcement for the Clive Churchill medal, it would be presented by his son. He stepped up to the microphone.

"This year's Clive Churchill medal goes to a man who is an exceptional player and leader. I would be hard pressed to think of a more deserving winner. Ladies and gentlemen, please congratulate the captain of today's winning team, and our winner— Nathan McKenzie."

Fuck! I'd had no idea I was a candidate for such a prestigious award. I pushed onto my feet from where I sat with teammates and made my way up to the platform. The medallion was draped around my neck to thunderous applause. After making a short speech, thanking my wife, parents, coach, teammates, and everyone who'd played a big part in my career, I returned to the team and received their congratulations. I was so damn proud of myself.

Next to be called up was the Captain of the Koalas. A $200,000 dollar runners-up cheque would be forthcoming. In his speech he thanked me and our team for a good, if not one-sided game and then thanked everyone who'd helped the Koalas to get to where they had. There was absolutely no reason for them to be ashamed, their achievements were much higher than anyone had expected, and they deserved to be proud of themselves.

After his speech, our men were called onto the dais to receive the grand final rings that were worth $10,000! We would receive $400,000 for our win which would add nicely to what we'd already won throughout the year.

I waited while everyone was called up on the dais, including coach and stepped up when I was called. After giving the winning captain's speech, I held the coveted Proven-Summons trophy high in the air. Camera flashes burned my eyeballs and after a few moments, the rest of the team joined me, and we were engulfed by colourful streamers. It was so much better than I dreamed.

After some celebration and autograph signings, we all made our way back to the sheds where the trophy was placed on a table and we all milled around, analysing, and dissecting the game.

Coach asked, or rather yelled over the noise, demanding that everyone sit, and once we settled, he spoke.

"I'll make this quick because Nate and I have our media conference in ten minutes. First of all, I am so fucking proud of you all. You played like the champions I know you are and blew the other team off the field. Next, Nate has something important to tell you all."

I stood and crossed to the centre of the room where I stood beside coach.

"Guys, you nailed it today and I'm so fucking proud of every one of you. It's a priviledge to have been your captain." I took a deep breath and glanced towards coach who gave me a reassuring nod. "This is hard and apart from Shauna, coach and management, no one else knows what I'm about to say."

Micah, a rather impatient individual, shouted across the room. "Get on with it, Nate, you're making me nervous."

"Firstly, you all know Shauna is four months pregnant with an unexpected but wonderful surprise. Thank fuck I had the sense to ask the woman to marry me before we found out because as some of you know, asking afterward does not go well."

"Rambling, Nate," Josh shouted.

"Okay. I had discussions with Shauna, Coach, and management a couple of months ago and I'm not re-signing with the club. At the press conference I'll be announcing my retirement."

Zane, Josh, and Micah, my three closest friends shot onto their feet and Micah exploded. "Bullshit, you're not ready for retirement and we can't play without you."

"I am very ready, Micah. I'm thirty-five-years old, my joints creak when I move and one muscle or another aches constantly. I've broken my right leg three times and it has more plates in it than a homemaker store. If I don't retire now, my kids will be pushing me around in a wheelchair. I'm done, guys. I worked hard for my law degree, and I want to make use of it before I die. I want weekends with Shauna and the kids."

My best friends, accepting and respecting what I was saying, stepped forward and pulled me into their arms before the rest of the team engulfed me in a group hug. I would miss seeing the men every day but knew they'd be friends for life. Hell, Shauna, and I had already asked Zane, Josh, and Micah, to be our kids' godfathers and they hadn't hesitated to accept. They'd had my back for sixteen years and I trusted them to have my kids'.

"Nate."

When coach spoke my name, the men released me and returned to sit down. He clapped me on the shoulder.

"Time for our press conference."

I picked up the trophy and walked with coach to the media room where I'd face the throng for the last time.

Then, it was home to celebrate alone with my gorgeous wife, the love of my life.

My Angel.

My TryAngel.

ABOUT THE AUTHOR

I'm an Australian author who writes in a variety of genres, including Western romance, historical romance, Gay Romance, and contemporary romance.

I have published over 60 books and novellas, many of which feature strong, independent heroines and rugged, alpha male heroes. Some of my popular series include the Outback Australia series and The Carter Brothers series.

My books are known for their well-researched historical details and vivid descriptions of the Australian landscape.

My work has garnered praise from readers and critics alike, and I have won several awards for my writing.

If you're interested in learning more about my books:

Linktree

https://linktr.ee/SusanHorsnell

Milton Keynes UK
Ingram Content Group UK Ltd.
UKHW020935231123
433129UK00016B/730